ICE AGE 4
CONTINENTAL DRIFT

MANNY'S BIG ADVENTURE

Written by J. E. Bright

First published in the UK
by HarperCollins Children's Books in 2012

1 3 5 7 9 10 8 6 4 2

978-0-00-792141-6

The HarperCollins website address is: www.harpercollins.co.uk

Printed and bound in UK

A loud rumble woke Manny the mammoth.

He checked on his wife, Ellie,

and his teenage daughter, Peaches.

Ellie was fine.

Peaches was missing!

Peaches had gone to the Falls, a teen hangout.
Manny was furious.

"You're overreacting," said Ellie.
"She won't be your little girl forever."
Manny said, "That's what worries me."

Her mother, Ellie,
was raised by possums.
She could hang from tree branches
by her tail.
Peaches also slept hanging upside down.
That's how her friend Louis,
a molehog, found her before
they went to the Falls.

"We shouldn't risk death," said Louis,
"so you can meet a cute mammoth."
Peaches said, "You can't live life
by playing it safe."
Manny snuck up behind Peaches.
"I know I would," he said.

"Dad," said Peaches, "don't be mad."

Manny grunted.

"You know how I feel

about you going to the Falls alone."

"She's not alone, sir," said Louis.

"You don't count," replied Manny.

Manny led Peaches away.

"We're going home," he said,

"where I can keep an eye on you."

Another rumble shook the ground,

scaring Louis back to his hole.

Despite her father's warnings,
Peaches and Louis snuck to the Falls.
They found a teen party!
"Look!" Peaches said to Louis.
"There's Ethan!"

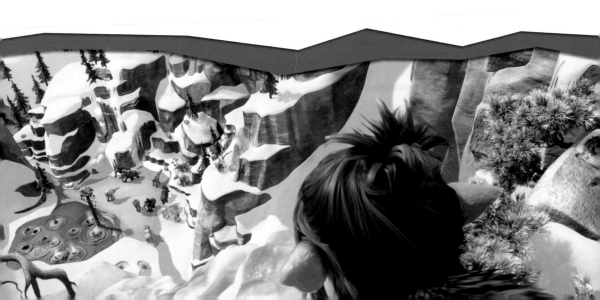

Peaches tripped, sliding down the ice!
She plummeted into the valley
and slammed into Ethan.
Their tusks tangled together.

At that moment, Manny appeared again.
"Am I interrupting something?"
he said angrily.
Peaches and Ethan tried
to untangle their tusks.

Manny yanked them apart.

"Keep away from my daughter!"

he said, growling at Ethan.

Then he told Peaches, "You're grounded!"

Embarrassed, Peaches stormed away.

Manny hurried after Peaches.
"Let's talk about this!" he said.
Peaches yelled, "I'm not a kid!
You can't control my life!"

That hurt Manny's feelings.
Peaches hurried away past Ellie.

"She doesn't mean it, honey,"
Ellie told Manny soothingly.

A huge rumble shook the earth.

Sid the sloth held his stomach.

"Whoa," he said. "Excuse me."

"I don't think that was you," said

Diego the saber-toothed tiger.

A crack split the icy ground
between Manny and his wife and daughter.
"Manny!" Ellie screamed. "No!"
"Peaches!" yelled Manny. "Get back!"

Sid and Diego grabbed onto Manny.
The ice shelf they stood on
slid into the water of the bay!
Manny ran along the edge of the ice,
looking for a place to jump.

"Hurry, Dad!" Peaches shouted.
Manny crouched to leap
across the icy water.
Diego stopped Manny from jumping.
"You won't make it!" said Diego.

The continent was crumbling!

"Go to the land bridge!" yelled Manny.

"You'll be safe on the other side!"

The broken ice shelf carried

Manny, Diego, and Sid out to sea.

"Daddy!" Peaches screamed.

Manny shouted, "I will find you!

No matter how long it takes."

"It's all my fault," wailed Peaches.
"If I had listened to him—"
Ellie said, "It's not your fault."
"But the last thing we did
was fight." Peaches sobbed.

"Your father is the toughest,
most stubborn mammoth I know,"
said Ellie. "He'll come back for us.
That's a promise."

Manny, Sid, and Diego floated
out onto the ocean.

They barely survived a wild storm.

"We have each other," said Sid.

"Things could be worse, right?"

Then they discovered a stowaway.

It was Sid's granny!

"Have you seen Precious?" asked Granny.

"You mean your imaginary pet?"
replied Diego. "No, I haven't."

Then Manny, Sid, and Diego
got into a sea battle with pirates.
They escaped on their melting iceberg.
"We'll never get home
on this thing," said Diego.

"Land!" cried Manny.

They had found an island . . .

but it was the pirate hideout!

They had to stop there—

the iceberg wouldn't last any longer.

On the pirate's island,
they discovered a fast current
called Switchback Cove.
"That's the way home!" said Manny.
Sid said, "But we need a ship."

Manny pointed at the pirates' ice ship.

Although the pirates swore revenge,

Manny, Diego, and Sid stole the ship!

The strong current carried them

back toward Manny's family.

After sailing a long time,
Manny spotted land again.
"We're almost home!" He cheered.
"I never doubted you," said Diego.
"Me neither," said Sid.

But the pirates got there first!

They grabbed Ellie and Peaches.

Manny thought all was lost.

Then Precious, Granny's real pet whale,

showed up to help save everybody!

Manny and his friends
and family sailed to a beautiful new land.
Manny, Ellie, and Peaches hugged.
"I love you, Dad," said Peaches.